Llama Llama
Shopping Drama

written and illustrated by
Anna Dewdney

Hodder
Children's
Books

Llama llama having fun.
Blocks and puzzles in the sun.

Time to shop!
It's Saturday!
Llama llama
wants to play.

First the
shopping,
then a treat.
Mama Llama
gets the seat.

Llama dreaming in the car –

Wake up!
Wake up!
Here we are!

Great big building,
great big signs.
Lots of aisles,
lots of lines.

Llama llama
out with Mama
shopping at the
Shop-O-Rama.

SALE!
50 % OFF
BLUE DOT

SALE!
SALE!
SALE!

Yucky music, great big feet.
Ladies smelling way too sweet.
Look at knees and stand in line.

SALE
20%OFF

Clearance sales
and discount buys.
What is little llama's size?
Try it on and take it off.
Pull and wiggle,
itch and cough.

Shirts and jackets,
pants and shoes.
Does this jumper
come in blue?
Brand-new socks
and underwear?

Llama llama
does not
care.

Cheesy Puffs and Oatie Crunch.
What would Llama like for lunch?
Llama llama doesn't know.
Llama llama wants to go.

Loaf of bread
and snacks to eat.
Llama llama wants his treat.
It's no fun at Shop-O-Rama.
Llama llama
MAD AT MAMA!

Flying pasta, spraying juice.

Paper towels rolling loose.

Coffee, bread and crisps galore.
Shoes and jumpers hit the floor.

CRASH the trolley
and SMASH the signs.
NO more waiting! NO more lines!
Out go socks and Cheesy Puffs. . . .

LLAMA
LLAMA,
THAT'S
ENOUGH!

Please stop fussing, little llama.
No more of this llama drama.
I think shopping's boring, too –
but at least I'm here with you.

Let's see if we can make this fun and get the llama shopping done.

Let's be a team
at Shop-O-Rama –
Llama llama shops with Mama!

Sweep up pasta,
mop up juice.
Wrap up towels
rolling loose.

Pick up puffs and find the socks.
Put the shoes back in the box.

Push the trolley
with Mama Llama,
almost done at Shop-O-Rama.

Time to leave.
The shopping's done.
No more waiting.
Time for fun.

Out to parking, not too far.
Where did Mama leave the car?

Snap the buckle, grab the box.
Put on brand-new
shoes and socks.

Say goodbye to Shop-O-Rama.
Llama Llama **LOVES** his mama.

For Cordelia, my shopping buddy.

LLAMA LLAMA SHOPPING DRAMA
Copyright © Anna Dewdney 2007
First published as *Llama Llama Mad at Mama* in 2007 by Viking,
a division of Penguin Young Readers Group, USA
First published in the UK in 2013 by Hodder Children's Books,
338 Euston Road, London, NW1 3BH
Hodder Children's Books Australia, Level 17/207 Kent Street, Sydney, NSW 2000

The right of Anna Dewdney to be identified as the author and illustrator of this Work has
been asserted by her in accordance with the Copyright, Designs and Patents Act 1988.

A catalogue record of this book is available from the British Library.

ISBN 978 1 444 91089 6
10 9 8 7 6 5 4 3 2 1

Printed in China

Hodder Children's Books is a division of Hachette Children's Books.
An Hachette UK Company.
www.hachette.co.uk